Unconditional Giving

The Power of Tolerance &
Forgiveness

Jaicy Ramsay

Transdependenz LLC

Ebook ISBN-13: 978-1-937145-07-1

Paperback ISBN-13: 978-1-937145-08-8

To my beloved teachers with love and gratitude!

⌘

"Kindness in words creates confidence.

Kindness in thinking creates profoundness.

Kindness in giving creates love"

- Lao Tzu

"Willy, you gotta grow up to be a mighty oak," Robert murmured as his bare hands gently felt the small tree's slender and somewhat pale-looking leaves. He noticed some cracks on the trunk and wondered if they were growth cracks or frost cracks.

"Where there is a will, there is a way!" he added while checking the loose alluvial topsoil around the pyramidal-looking young tree with his hands. He always ensured that the soil above the roots was moist but not fully wet.

After his wife's departure, Robert had moved into a small townhome near the suburbs of southern New Jersey to live close to his son, Albert, who resided a couple of blocks down Liberty Street. One of the first things Robert did as soon as he had moved in was to get a young willow oak (also known as peach oak or pin oak) tree from the city's Urban Forestry Advisory Council (UFAC) and plant it in front of his house.

The UFAC was encouraging the residents to grow native plants to add ornamental value to the town's unique historic setting. He, with some help from Albert, had gently pulled out the small tree from its container and placed it in the planting hole.

At the end of the successful transplantation efforts, Robert had exclaimed, "Hail Willy, the mighty oak!" and since then, the willow oak in front of his house had come to be known as "Willy."

The young tree had seemed to be doing well for a year or so. But, then last year, it had leafed out late on the top branch, and some of its branches had lost leaves. Robert had become very concerned seeing some patches of discoloration on the bark and an area of apparent sponginess that the tree had developed.

"Could it be canker? Slim flux?" His mind had been fully occupied with thoughts of Willy as he went about his daily routine. As soon as he would get out of the bed a little before dawn, he would rush out of the house to check if Willy had showed signs of recovery. He initially had tried some standard remedies based on the little arboricultural training he had had from his father. But Willy had seemed to get worse.

Finally, after spending many sleepless nights thinking about how to help his sick friend, Willy, he consulted the local arborists and tree doctors and tried out different treatments on Willy. But none of them worked. To him, Willy appeared to be dying cell by cell, a sight that he could not bear to see.

Then one day, a life-saving remedy popped out of a book Robert was casually reading when he was waiting at the local natural therapist's office for his annual health check-up. The book hailed the properties of cow manure for its rich micronutrients and its usefulness as a natural fertilizer for trees with its excellent balance of nitrogen (N), phosphoric acid (P), and potash (K). Although somewhat skeptical at first, Robert nonetheless decided to give it a try having found no other panacea for his ailing friend.

Much to his amazement and joy, Willy recovered within a month of treating the soil with the cow manure he had collected from the local organic dairy farm. Since then, the application of cow manure to the soil had become part of his tree caring routine.

Just as the moon develops day after day in its waxing phase, Willy, at a rapid growth rate, developed into a tall tree with a densely branched rounded crown and a massive girth in just over a decade.

No one else took as much interest as Robert in watching Willy mature. He could observe and remember every single detail about Willy's growth: the glossy light-green leaves that terminated with a hair-like tip, the distinct venation on the leaf bottom, the first appearance of long and slender yellowish-green catkins (male flowers) hanging down at the tip of the branches, the pistillate (female) flowers appearing in small clusters near the junction of leaf stems, the turning of smooth, light-reddish colored bark into roughened narrow ridges as he grew old, etc.

Willy's stately features and majestic appearance earned him a reputation of becoming an important landmark in the neighborhood.

Having been a farmer all his life, Robert had a unique way of communicating his thoughts to the plants and trees which only they understood. And he knew they understood him.

"Whoever said trees are inert doesn't understand the symbiotic relationship between Mother Nature and us. If you love them and are willing to hear them carefully, they will speak with you," Robert would tell his neighbor when they went together for an early morning brisk walk in the empty street.

He always treated the plants and trees as living persons with feelings and would never get tired of staying around them.

Over the years, Robert and Willy shared a certain friendly intimacy that no one else, except they, were privy to. Although Robert treated Willy like his best friend, Willy always considered Robert as his master and held a reverential friendly attitude towards him.

Robert would often sit under the willow oak and play on his baroque oboe for his friend while observing the sun rays peep through the leaves with a kaleidoscope effect.

During the late afternoon hours, he would lie on a hammock and talk to Willy about Albert's newlywed wife Lisa and her awe-inspiring paintings while relishing Willy's branches dance to the soothing breeze.

Sometimes, he would doze off sitting underneath Willy's cooling shade while reading a novel by Somerset Maugham or listening to Mozart on the gramophone.

Albert and Lisa regularly spent their weekend at Robert's home. Lisa was fond of her father-in-law's vegetarian recipes, and they had fun cooking together for the family.

Sometimes, Lisa's sister, her family, and relatives joined in, and soon enough the lawn under Willy's widespread branches became a hot weekend picnic spot, especially during summer.

Willy's trunk and other nearby bushes offered an ideal opportunity for the kids to play hide-and-seek. The adults took turns in using the rope tree swing with a wooden seat that Robert had carefully set up.

During one such picnic day, Albert seemed distant as he was very upset with a co-worker's misdemeanor at the workplace and was contemplating some sort of tit-for-tat. From Albert's grunted looks, Robert could sense that something was not right with his son and gently prodded him.

Very reluctantly, Albert disclosed his mind to his father when they went for shopping at the local farm market in the evening.

As he had always experienced before, within a few minutes of discussion with his father, his heart was pacified and he somewhat regretted his revengeful attitude he had held towards the co-worker.

Robert had shown to him how trees like Willy never retaliate but always do good even to those who treat them with disrespect, insult them, or hurt them.

"The tree stands and gives shade until the end even to the very person who is cutting it down." These words of Robert's awakened a higher sense in Albert, and he thanked his father for always being there for him.

Whether it was the death of a relative or the arrival of a newborn in the family, Robert would speak out his heart to Willy. Some of the happiest news Robert had ever shared with Willy was regarding the birth of his grandson, Roger.

"Aren't you excited, silly-Willy?" His joy knew no bounds when he told Willy that Albert and Lisa would be bringing in Roger the following weekend. As soon as they arrived, Robert received the baby in his hands and went out to show the little one to Willy.

"He looks a lot like you, Robert," Willy commented as he gently shook his branches as if wanting to laugh loudly.

While many in the neighborhood appreciated the willow oak's fine foliage and amazing winter features, Robert saw something deeper. He seemed to be deriving newer and newer inspirations from Willy that he was fond of sharing with his near and dear ones in the form of poems and essays.

One particular poem that he shared during a family dinner in thoughts of separation from Willy touched everyone's heart:

Oh! Tell me, where is Willy, the mighty oak?

Down to earth, rising up to the sky

Humility are his roots spread far and wide

Resilient in the face of changing seasons, an emblem of tolerance

Intolerant of another's sorrow, his heart is white!

Oh! Tell me, where is Willy, the mighty oak?

Selflessness and compassion, his graceful beauty

Providing shelter to one and all, he goes beyond the call of duty

A miracle to behold, teaching us endless lessons

He lives forever and ever in the heart of his admirer!

"Time flies so fast, doesn't it?" Robert said as he cleared the beads of sweat on his wrinkled forehead with the back of his right palm. He wore a pullover sweatshirt and rain boots and knelt on the ground as he transferred the last set of garden mums from their pot into the soil in front of his house. It was mid-August and the sun was shining bright. Next to him stood the seven-year-old curious-looking Roger who held a plastic sand shovel in his hand with a small rolling lawn cart next to him. Robert turned and smiled at Roger who shrugged his shoulder and squinted his eyes.

Robert said, "Ohhh! Yeah," and turned back to leveling the soil around the plant with his hands.

"Now, help this old man to stand straight," Robert said with his right hand outstretched. Roger dropped the shovel and tried to pull his grandpa's hand towards him. Robert pretended to get up by holding Roger's hand, but finally pulled Roger down towards him and made him sit on his lap. Both of them looked at Willy and laughed like a drain.

Although Roger apparently stayed with his parents, he practically grew up with his grandpa. Naturally, he imbibed the same caring attitude as his grandpa towards plants and trees and manifested a high level of maturity and wisdom that one wouldn't expect to see in a nine-year-old. He was at total ease in speaking the language of Willy, his grandpa's best friend.

At 80, Robert had the appetite and gusto of a young man, but more recently, he was finding it difficult to concentrate on a task for a long time and often gasped for breath after his morning walks. Albert and Lisa had put up their house for sale and had permanently come to live with Robert. As Robert had found it unbearable to cope with the thought of leaving Willy and moving into Albert's home, they agreed to come and stay with him.

Of course, Roger was the happiest in all this as he could now be around his grandpa the whole day.

As the fall season progressed into winter and with the increase of cold winter winds, Willy shed all the leaves on his branches and stood grave on the frozen top soil. His master and friend had not come out the whole day yesterday, which was quite unusual for him.

Through the large window he could see Albert, Lisa, and Roger gathered in that room where Robert was lying still in the bed with his eyes closed. The night before he had looked at Willy through the window and had lifted his hand from the bed half-away in a waving motion. Little did Willy realize that his master was wishing him a final goodbye!

It was an unrecoverable loss for both Willy and Roger. They slowly got over it by conversing about Robert and his noble qualities from what they knew of him in their own way.

With the arrival of spring, leaf buds began to appear on Willy's branches, and as the temperatures rose, the buds grew to be leaves, and soon enough he regained his full, leafy canopies. The bountiful production of shallow-capped acorns was once again in full swing. Blue jays and red-headed woodpeckers became regular visitors while grackles and northern flickers began building their nests on Willy's branches.

And Roger's school was in session.

"Do you want to see deer?" Willy asked Roger as he played on the tree swing in the evening.

"Deer! I would love to...I have only seen them in pictures," Roger exclaimed. "But how can *you* show me one?" He was surprised at Willy's proposal.

"How about you sneak out of your bed and quietly come to me a little after midnight?" Willy tried to tempt him.

"Really! I can't believe it." Roger's mouth was agape.

"Yes, they find my acorns delicious. They generally come in a batch of two or three when the whole town is asleep," Willy said to Roger.

"Wow...amazing!...I'll definitely be there tonight...Don't let them escape, please," Roger thanked Willy. "Okay, I got to go and do my homework now...see you tonight!" His eyes sparkled as he went inside the house.

Roger couldn't sleep that night. He was not confident about his ability to sleep for a few hours and get up at midnight. Setting up the alarm clock to ring at midnight would wake up his parents and sabotage his plan. He turned towards the window and pulled his blanket up to his neck. He closed his eyes pretending to have fallen asleep when his parents came to kiss him good night. They switched off the lights and went out leaving his bedroom door partially closed.

Roger kept imagining how the deer might look and tried to recollect the pictures he had seen in books. "The white-tailed deer is the most common in New Jersey. An adult male deer is called a buck and a female deer is known as a doe. A fawn is a young deer, typically under the age of one year," he recollected from his science class.

Right around 10:00 PM, Roger fell asleep thinking and thinking. Tap…tap…tap, he strained to open his eyelids as he thought someone was knocking on his window. Not wanting to be disturbed, he turned over and closed his eyes.

"Oh…oh…." He sprang up and sat on the bed as he remembered Willy's offer to show him deer a little after midnight. He stared at the ticking clock. It was already 12:30 AM.

"Oh, my God! The deer would have come and gone. How long could Willy keep them? He must have waited for me." Roger was upset with himself as he quietly pulled the windowpane up and squeezed himself through it to jump out on the grass.

"I am so sorry, Willy. I wanted to be awake...but then…. Have the deer come and gone?" Roger tried to explain himself.

"Shhhh!" Willy hushed him through the rustling of leaves in the soft breeze. "They can be here anytime now…. Go and hide behind your father's car. You'll be able to see them as they feed on my acorns," Willy directed him.

Roger followed Willy's advice feeling relieved that he had not missed the opportunity to see white-tailed deer up close.

He ducked behind his father's Chevrolet Cavalier and saw through the transparent windows. Nothing happened for a while. He had not realized how silent the whole town was at this time of the night. He noticed the occasional movement of automobiles on the street in front of his house leading to the county road. The nocturnal crickets were chirping away. But, no deer in sight.

"Maybe they could sense some potential danger and cancelled their trip," Roger thought.

Then all of a sudden, three deer, including a fawn, jumped out of the bushes from nowhere. The deer parents seemed to carefully guard the fawn as they kept close vigilance of the surroundings and moved towards Willy. The young fawn was fearless and agile. He became excited as soon as he spotted the acorns strewn on the ground and ran for it. After feasting on the acorns for a while, they quietly took off and went out of sight as discreetly as they appeared on the scene.

Roger was amused by the whole event he had just witnessed and profusely thanked Willy for the close-up deer show. Imitating the deer, he jumped back into his room through the window and sneaked into his bed.

"See you in the evening," Roger said to Willy as he rushed out of his house in the morning to reach the bus stop two blocks down the street where the school bus would come and pick him up every day.

"Don't forget your lunchbox pack." Lisa came running behind Roger and pushed it inside his backpack.

After a busy day at school, Roger returned back to his home, ate some snacks, completed his homework assignments, and came out to be with Willy as he had done every day. He came close and sat resting his back against Willy's trunk and facing the street.

Vehicles passed by at 35 miles per hour, including a few large trucks carrying furniture. The traffic had grown exponentially in the last few years, not so much due to the economic growth in that locality, but because the paved street in front of Robert's house became an important link to the county road leading to the beltway.

A cloud of dense smoke hung over the street amidst moving traffic and columns of smoke rose from the chimneys of a distant cement plant which reminded Roger of his grandpa.

"You see, Roger," Robert had said pointing at the smoke and the soot, "that is our gift to the environment and each other. And we don't care because we know that trees like Willy are there to absorb all that poison within themselves and release useful oxygen into the atmosphere."

"Won't it hurt them?" Roger had innocently asked.

"Yes, it does. But it is their nature to never complain about anything but go on doing good to others even at the cost of risking their lives. That doesn't mean that we should take advantage of them," Robert had replied.

The honk of a car around the intersection broke Roger's meditation. "You know, Willy, today our science teacher talked about you in class," he said to Willy with a smile.

"Really? I hope it was not all that bad," Willy said.

"I couldn't believe that you grew out so big and tall out of those tiny acorns!" he exclaimed looking at the acorns strewn on the ground.

"We are tiny, but God is great, Roger," Willy said feeling a little shy.

The old lady from the neighboring house waved at Roger as she walked her Yorkshire Terrier puppy on the sidewalk. The puppy stopped smelling the sidewalk for a while and curiously looked at the young boy and the tree with her ears pointing to the sky. "Wov...wov...wov," she started barking at them in great excitement and wanted to run towards them.

"C'mon, Amy...let's go...let's go." The old lady pulled the dog leash towards her. "She is a little restless today," she turned back and said to Roger apologetically as she went past them.

"So, what do you want to become, Roger, when you grow up?" Willy asked.

Roger thought for a while and looked at the sky. "May be a farmer? Doctor?...." Willy thought he should give him some options.

"I want to become like you, Willy," Roger said resting his head on the trunk gently. "Always kind to others…whether I become a doctor or engineer…." he added.

"No doubt, you are the grandson of Robert the Wise," Willy said moving his branches gently with the late afternoon breeze. "But, you can become more than me," Willy added.

"Hmmm….How so?" Roger was puzzled.

"Let me narrate you the story of LeRoy that your grandpa once told me. This LeRoy used to be a wealthy man. But, somehow he became afflicted with a serious skin disease. Not wanting to disturb others, he moved out of town and lived near the forest on the city outskirts. Due to skin eruptions, his body was infected with wounds oozing out puss and blood. Naturally, maggots and worms started attacking them for food. But LeRoy used to be so kind to them that he considered letting his brothers, the maggots and worms, feed on his wounds as the best thing he could do with his body in that condition. When they would fall off, he would gently pick them up and place them back on his wounds thinking that he should not deprive them of their food." Willy became emotional as he remembered Robert's voice.

"Roger, there is only so much I can do for others....My capacity is limited," Willy said to Roger.

"But you have been endowed with the ability to freely move and much more...use your gifts to help your fellow beings...become a moving mighty oak...go wherever there is scorching sunlight and offer your shade and shelter there," Willy appealed to him.

"This is the kind of person your grandpa wanted you to become...a moving mighty oak." Saying those words, Willy tried to gently stroke Roger's head by showering some leaves.

"Yes, I will…." Roger looked at Willy with glossy eyes.

"Roger…Roger….c'mon….it's time for dinner." Lisa came out and held the front door half-open indicating to Roger to get inside quickly.

Roger kept turning back to look at Willy as he inched forward into the house with his mommy.

The next day broke with some mild showers. The sky was overcast. Cars, trucks, and vans drove by the street as usual. Squirrels were busy playing and smelling the acorns. "What a nice day!" Willy thought as his leaves fluttered in the wind.

A truck drove past Willy and came to a standstill half a block down the street. The side of the truck bore the words: "Cut-n-Prune Tree Services."

Four men dressed in work apparel got out of the truck and approached Willy. Two of them wore bib overalls and safety vests while the other two wore cargo pants and quilted nylon vests.

The same men had come a few days ago with an inch tape and other measurement tools. They had measured the tree's girth and surveyed its branches and went around to see how far it was spread. After a while, they had gotten into their truck and driven away.

The same crew now assembled in front of Willy with a singular mission and Willy already got a clue of it.

One of them smoked a cigar, wore a helmet, and carried a chainsaw.

"It ain't gonna be so easy to bring this monster down," he spoke with a Texan accent as he moved the cigar from one side of his mouth to the other.

One among the four men appeared to be young and sympathetic as he said, "It is not infested with insects. It doesn't appear to be a hazard and it is rock solid all the way through. I think we should feel sorry that we have to do this to a healthy tree just because it is somehow in the way."

The man with the helmet, who seemed to be the leader of the crew, discarded that suggestion as he took a small axe from his heavy-duty tool belt and stuck it on the trunk and said, "Enough of that Mr. Shakespeare. Let's get to work."

After a few minutes, two massive chippers and truck-mounted containers arrived on the spot.

Willy understood that his time had come.

The city officials had been contemplating this idea for a while. The paved street in front of Roger's house had become an important link to the county road leading to the beltway. Consequently, the traffic had been steadily increasing over the years, and now the City wanted to widen the street to accommodate the increased traffic. It was no surprise that their eyes fell on Willy who had been stationed there for a while right next to the street.

Many residents, including Albert and his wife, were opposed to the idea and tried to dissuade the public officials from embarking on this destruction program. They had even argued from the point of aesthetics and how the city's unique historical setting would be blemished by the removal of the royal oak tree.

But finally, the city's economic and political interests had over-ruled aesthetics concerns, and they had decided to proceed with the street widening project.

Cut-n-Prune Tree Services got the contract to bring the tree down as they had the reputation of being the best tree fellers in the town.

The destruction of Willy was imminent.

Roger had been watching the commotion from inside through his window. "What's going on, Mom?" he now anxiously asked looking at Lisa. His father had left town a couple of days ago on an urgent work-related trip.

"Well…they have come to…they have come to…." she swallowed the lump in her throat as she bit her lower lip.

"Come to ….What?" Roger gently shook his mom as he looked outside the window.

"They have come to bring down our Willy." She burst into tears as she he held his face in her palms and closed her eyes, not having the courage to look at him.

"What??? Why??? What is Willy's fault?" Roger couldn't believe his mom's words.

"There is no fault on his part. His only fault is that he happens to be in the way of their progress and development." Lisa could hardly speak.

Roger pushed his mom back and ran to the door. He opened the latch and hopped into the grass and scurried towards Willy. The tree-cutting crew were at the other side of the street to estimate the potential impact on the surroundings as the trunk fell.

"Willy…" Roger mildly gasped for breath and tried to tightly embrace Willy's trunk with tears in his eyes.

"Very nice to see you, Roger," Willy welcomed him.

"Willy, they have come to get you…" Roger was gasping for breath.

"We all have to go one day, Roger. That time has come for me now," Willy replied calmly.

"No, no. It is not possible…it is not possible," Roger shook his head and tried to climb on Willy. "Willy, with all your might, you can drop a branch or two and scare them away. They will never come back." Roger pleaded with Willy in his childish innocence.

"Is that going to change anything, Roger?" Willy looked at Roger with compassion. "They think I am getting in their way and want to get rid of me. So, I should cooperate to make it easier for them," Willy spoke gently.

"But…but…" Roger was speechless.

"Roger, I am grateful to you for your love," Willy interrupted and continued. "But, please try to understand. We trees are meant to serve others with our every breath and as long as we stand. Today, these men have approached me and it is my bounden duty to provide them shade and shelter and give them whatever they want from me....even if that means giving up my life." Willy caressed Roger's hair with the tip of his branches.

"But, they are not going to ask you anything….they are going to kill you…whether or not you cooperate," Roger kept repeating amidst his tears.

"It doesn't matter, Roger. It doesn't matter. Whether they have come to nourish me or kill me, I should do good to them…whatever I can within my capacity. Please don't think ill of them," Willy said.

"But, what about the squirrels and the deer? Where will they go now to get their acorns? What about the blue jays, the woodpecker, and the grackles….where will they all go now for shelter?" Roger sounded a bit angry due to uncontrollable emotions.

"If not me, they will find another willow oak, Roger. I am not indispensable!" Willy replied.

After having exhausted all his arguments to save his friend, Roger resigned to the idea that he would not be able to see Willy anymore.

No more of those casual late afternoon talks resting his back on Willy's trunk after he returned from his school. No more discussions about his grandpa while he played in the rope tree swing hanging from Willy's main branch. His tears were uncontrollable as he mumbled "Willy...Willy."

"Now, please go back to your room because I don't want you to get hurt while they cut me down," Willy pleaded with Roger. "Lisa and Albert love you very much. Please take good care of them always. I have every hope that you'll grow up to be a selfless and compassionate being, just like your noble grandpa. I wish you the very best." With those final words, Willy became grave and silent.

Roger stood there motionless. He looked at Willy from top to bottom and caressed Willy's trunk with his hands.

The tree crew returned to the spot and started making preparations. They cordoned off the area with barriers and yellow caution tapes.

With great reluctance, Roger turned towards his home and took one step at a time. As he approached the steps leading to the entrance, a sudden gust of wind blew across his face. A sheet of paper from his study room flew through the window and fluttered down on Roger's face as he stood on the low-height entrance stairs. Roger seemed to recognize the handwritten sheet of paper as he carefully picked it up, unfolded it, and read it:

Oh! Tell me, where is Willy, the mighty oak?

Selflessness and compassion, his graceful beauty

Providing shelter to one and all, he goes beyond the call of duty

A miracle to behold, teaching us endless lessons

He lives forever and ever in the heart of his admirer!

He felt that his grandpa was speaking to him at this critical moment, urging him to do something to save Willy. Roger read those words again and again until they became etched in his heart. He then wiped his tears, turned back and walked towards Willy with resolute determination.

"Willy, they will have to first get me before they can touch you," Roger stood close to Willy's trunk facing the tree fellers who were ready with their chainsaws.

"What's up, boy? If you need to take a picture or two before we cut it down, go ahead. We have few minutes", the man with the Texan accent spoke.

"Sir, please hear me out. This tree has done nothing except to do good to others. Why do you want to cut it down for no reason? Is it not our bounden duty to protect, and not exploit, our younger brothers and sisters?" Roger appealed to the leader of the crew.

The crew leader's face became red with anger, but he controlled his emotions and leaned towards Roger.

"Look, young boy. It'll be just a matter of hours. Why don't you go inside your home and watch a cartoon or play with your dog? When you come back after a few hours, we'll be gone...so will this tree be... clean and smooth. Does that sound like a plan?" he blew some smoke from his cigar as he chuckled.

Roger coughed a little and cleared his throat.

"My dear Sir, please listen to me carefully. This is my beloved friend, Willy. You will have to first sever my head from my body before you can touch his trunk. I'll fight until my last breath to protect him and save him from you," Roger spoke firmly as he tightly folded his arms across his chest.

The old lady from the neighboring house, who was watching the scene for a while, went inside and gave a ring to her niece, a reporter working for the local TV news channel.

"I think you may have some breaking news here, but you need to come right away," she briefly summarized what had happened and hung the phone quickly to catch up with the proceedings.

"What is this nonsense! I don't have to hear a sermon from this lil' chap. We are already late. Go and call his mother," the leader ordered one of the crew man to knock on the entrance door.

Lisa came out and tried to comprehend the situation fully. She had been waiting for Roger to return inside after saying goodbye to Willy. But, now, she saw Roger in a defiant mood standing close to Willy posing a severe obstacle to the tree fellers. Internally, she admired her young son's courage to stand up for the right cause, but she feared that harm may come his way.

Roger's eyes met his mothers' with an assuring glance.

"Mom, Willy has selflessly served us all these years. Now, it is our turn," he said.

"Ma'am, can you please take your boy inside or take him out on a ride? We have to get going," the irritated leader turned towards Lisa and spoke as he prepared to start the chainsaw motor.

"No, I cannot. He will not listen to me," Lisa said without looking at him.

"I think it is best if you all go back now and report to the City officials what you just witnessed," she added.

A white remote minivan belonging to the local TV news channel entered the street at high speed and came to a screeching halt before hitting the yellow ribbons that proclaimed the designated work area. A television reporter and a cameraman hopped out of the remote broadcasting van and rushed to the spot.

"What the hell is going on here? Why are you people here?" the leader was furious.

"Sir, please mind your language. You are about to go on the air," the news reporter said after she stood before the camera with the leader, Roger and Willy to her back.

In less than a minute, she summarized the City's considerations and its decision to cut down the tree in spite of the protests lodged by the local residents.

"In an interesting turn of events, a 9-year old boy is putting up a severe challenge to the City's order to bring down the willow oak tree," she added as the camera followed Roger, Willy, and finally the leader.

The leader of the tree-cutting crew from Cut-n-Prune Tree Services appeared to have lost it as his eyes were bloodshot and his lips quivered with rage.

"This is total nonsense. Why are you people making a big fuss over a heap of wood? I can't believe this. I have felled so many trees in my career. Nobody has ever stopped me like this……I am here to decimate this stupid tree to pieces. And, I am going to smack this impudent lad if he doesn't listen to me," he said pointing his chainsaw at Roger.

He realized his blunder when he saw the camera zoom in on him. He initially ran towards the cameraman with the idea of destroying the equipment with his chainsaw, but later held himself, rushed towards his truck and took off without waiting for his crew members.

The short live news clip created a sensation among the city residents. Everyone, including the industrialists and the environmental activists, sympathized with Roger's cause.

News columns and articles were published in praise of young Roger's divine qualities and denounced the human arrogance towards Mother Nature. Flags and street banners began to grow everywhere in the city announcing, "Save Willy, the Mighty Oak". The environmental activists hosted a rally through the city and started a petition to Save Willy.

Roger and Willy became the talk of the town.

Initially, the City tried to pacify the residents by advertising the economic advantages that would come about through the completion of the street widening project.

"There is always some sacrifice involved in achieving a greater cause," the mayor had said on TV. But, it didn't touch the hearts of the residents.

As the resistance from the residents grew stronger and stronger to the street widening project, the City finally changed its mind and made an official announcement to spare Willy and find an alternative link to the county road.

The mayor declared Willy a historic landmark and personally congratulated Roger for his chivalrous act and selflessness.

As far as Roger was concerned, he was happy to be with Willy again!

********The End********

A Special Note from the Author

Thank you very much for reading this book.

Would you please kindly take a minute or two to leave your review here?: http://amzn.to/1KdldQ7

Even a few words is sufficient and is greatly appreciated!

About the Author

Jaicy Ramsay is a writer, author, teacher, and an engineer. He is always eager to learn about healthy and wholesome lifestyles, habits, and attitudes and sharing with others.

He specializes in the art of conveying motivational themes and inspiring messages in an easy-to-read manner through the powerful medium of storytelling.

Also By Jaicy Ramsay

Every Moment is A New Beginning: The Power of Positivity and Gratitude

http://amzn.to/1Br35z4

More often than not, life presents us with seemingly insurmountable challenges. You try hard, but they seem to grow bigger and bigger. What do you do when you apparently have all cards stacked against you in the game of life?

The good news: there is a very simple time-tested solution to this age-old complex problem

Read *Every Moment is a New Beginning* to:

- Realize how little things can make a big positive difference in your life

- Grow your respect and appreciation for even the most insignificant of things

- Understand how you can always choose to be happy if you want to

- Be in the present and leave behind your past

- Overcome negative thoughts through positive meditation

Written in the form of a contemporary self-improvement parable with colorful illustrations, this short book is a motivational guide to positive thinking and cultivating an attitude of gratitude amidst life's toughest struggles.

Meet Alissa, a typical, young working woman who is suddenly overwhelmed with real-life challenges that add up one after another to the point of threatening her very existence.

What happens to her next?

Apply the simple principles contained in this book and experience a new beginning in your life right this moment!

Available at: http://amzn.to/1Br35z4